A special dedication of thanks.
To my brothers Willie, Tyrone, and Gerald Henson.
Because of your initial artistic aspirations which I always
admired, I learned, discovered and found the artist within me.

A special thanks!

To order additional copies of this book, contact:
Xlibris
1-888-795-4274
www.Xlibris.com
Orders@Xlibris.com

# Discover the inspirational magic created from smiles through the guidance of Mr. Sunny Sunshine.

Looking for a Smile.
Written and Illustrated
by
Dwayne S. Henson

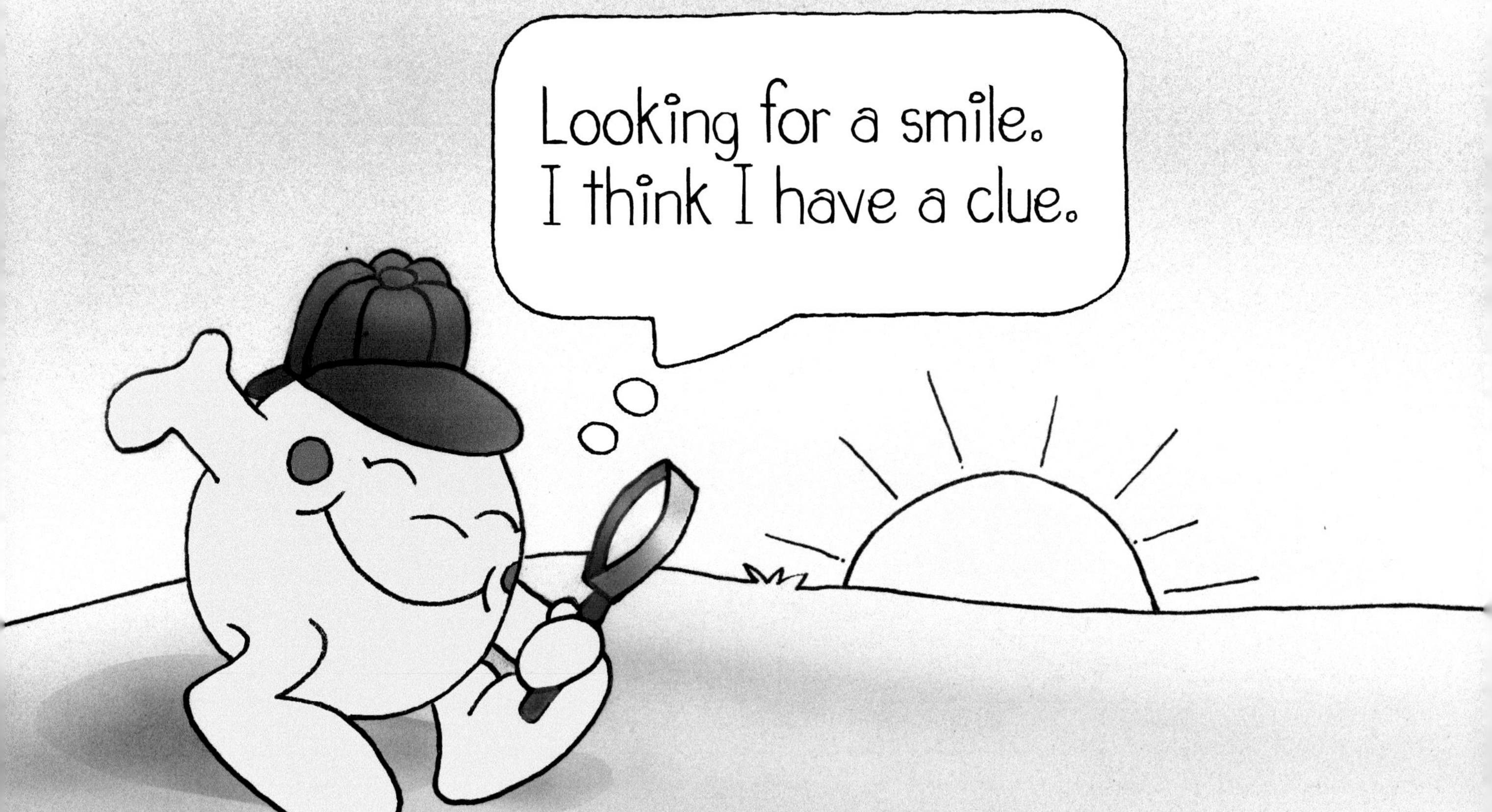
Looking for a smile.
I think I have a clue.

Maybe I'll just pole vault over to Hawaii. I might get lucky.

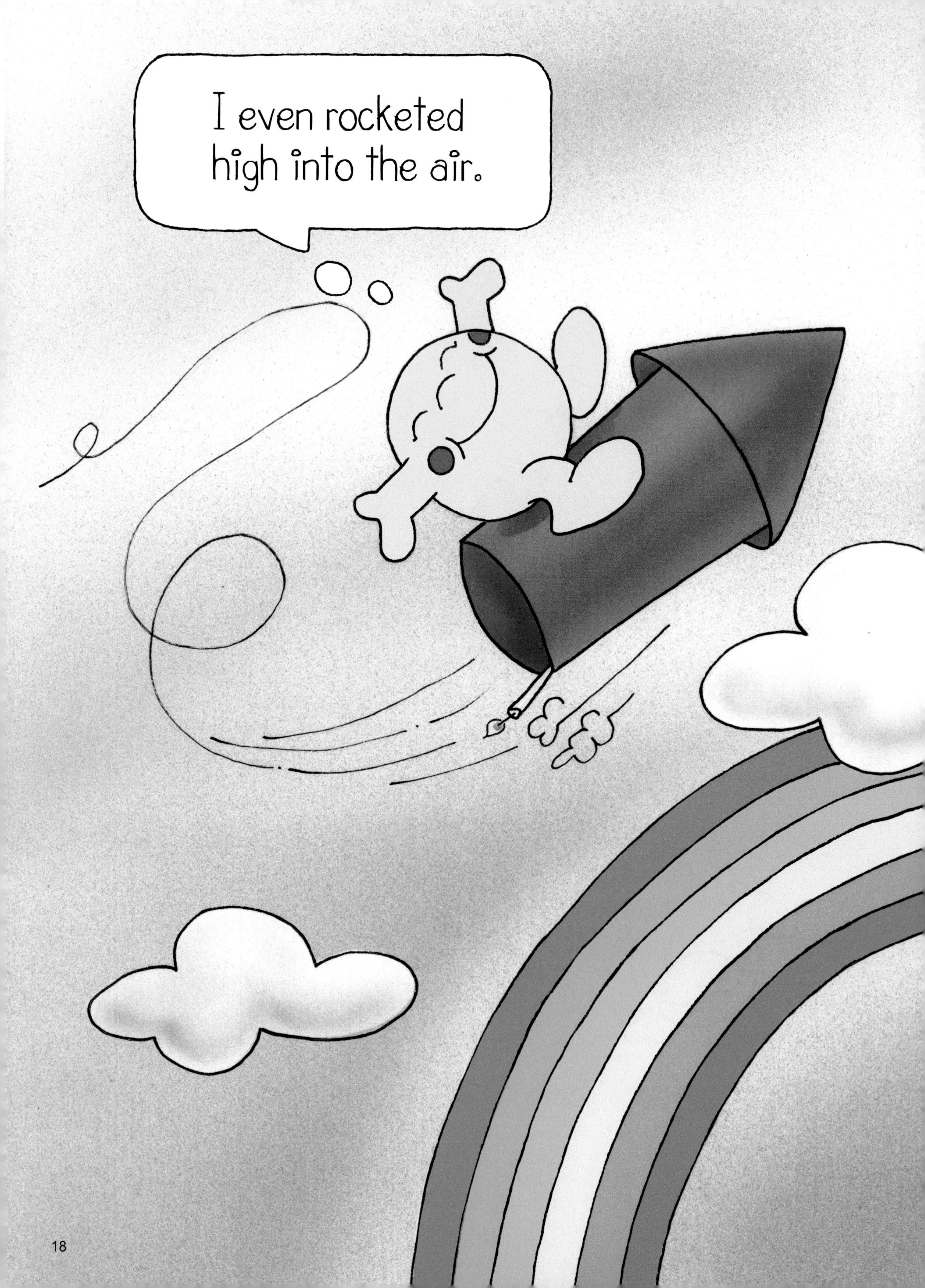
I even rocketed high into the air.

"It's a smile!" it's a smile, staring me right in the face. It's a smile in such an easy place. I don't know how I ever could have missed it or why I even started on this silly wild goose chase. But I am happy and glad that I solved the case. Now, I know how to find a smile without even a clue. I hope you can too. Smile, smile, smile and smile!

A special offer from
the author / illustrator of the
Mr. Sunny Sunshine books
Dwayne S. Henson

Here's my special offer.
Two preschool educational
books combined in one at
one regular sales price.

For more information on this special offer
and other Mr. Sunny Sunshine books
Contact Xlibris at: 1-888-795-4274

## Dwayne S. Henson
## Creator of Mr. Sunny Sunshine™

My gift that I would like to share with others is to inspire those who are in need of a smile and to educate others of the positive inspirational value that smiles provide in our society.

With Mr. Sunny Sunshine™ as my tool in this never ending educational smile-based journey, I aim to demonstrate how smiles can be utilized in so many positive encouraging ways such as to inspire, motivate, educate as well as to entertain. How Mr. Sunny Sunshine™ creates smiles and shares them with others, I truly believe, are some of the fascinating trademark dynamics of this inspiring smile making concept.

As you may come to discover there's more inspirational magic behind a smile than what we generally see.

From this unique unit of books you'll learn how and why Mr. Sunny Sunshine™ took it upon himself to create more smiles and inspiration all over the world. Along with this you'll also be provided with a one-of-a-kind, entertaining, smile-based education and much, much, more.

There's a lot to uncover and learn about a smile. I invite you to journey along to see how truly motivating a smile can be.

I certainly hope you enjoy my Mr. Sunny Sunshine™ books as much as I did creating them for others to share. I look forward to creating lots more smiles for many of years to come.

Sincerely, Dwayne S. Henson... Prince of happiness, King of smiles.

Printed in the United States
By Bookmasters